WHEN I GET BIGGER

BY
MERCER MAYER

A Random House PICTUREBACK® Book

Random House 🏠 New York

When I Get Bigger book, characters, text, and images © 1999 Mercer Mayer. LITTLE CRITTER, MERCER MAYER'S LITTLE CRITTER, and MERCER MAYER'S LITTLE CRITTER and Logo are registered trademarks of Orchard House Licensing Company. All rights reserved. Published in the United States by Random House Children's Books, a division of Random House, Inc., New York. Originally published in 1999 by Golden Books Publishing Company, Inc. PICTUREBACK, RANDOM HOUSE, and the Random House colophon are registered trademarks of Random House, Inc.
www.randomhouse.com/kids
Educators and librarians, for a variety of teaching tools, visit us at
www.randomhouse.com/teachers
Library of Congress Control Number: 82-84110
ISBN-10: 0-307-11943-2   ISBN-13: 978-0-307-11943-8
Printed in the United States of America
40 39 38
First Random House Edition 2006

When I get bigger
I'll be able to do
lots of things.

I'll wait until the light is green.
Then I'll look both ways for cars
before I cross the street.

I'll have my own watch and I'll tell everyone what time it is.

I'll go on a bus
to Grandma and
Grandpa's.

When I get bigger I'll have
a real leather football...

...my own radio, and a pair of
superpro roller skates.

I'll have a two-wheeler and a paper route.
I'll make lots of money.

At the playground
I'll help the little kids
on the swings.

I'll pick out
my own boots
at the shoe store.

I'll make a phone call
and dial it myself.

I'll order something from a catalog...

...and it will come in the mail.

When I get bigger I'll camp out in the backyard all night long.

Or I'll stay up to
see the end of the
late movie.
Even if I get sleepy,
I won't go to bed.

But right now I have to go to bed…

…because Mom and Dad say…

...I'm not bigger yet.